This Little Tiger book belongs to:

Harry
Blbdurst
a ne

For my own chicks, Kate and Anna. Love always – E B

For Lucie, thanks for all your support.
Don't get pooped on! – M C

LITTLE TIGER PRESS

1 The Coda Centre, 189 Munster Road, London SW6 6AW

www.littletigerpress.com

First published in Great Britain 2012

This edition published 2012

Text copyright © Elizabeth Baguley 2012

Illustrations copyright © Mark Chambers 2012

Elizabeth Baguley and Mark Chambers have asserted their rights

to be identified as the author and illustrator of this work

under the Copyright, Designs and Patents Act, 1988

ISBN 978-1-84895-489-2 • LTP/1400/0396/0412

Printed in China

2 4 6 8 10 9 7 5 3 1

Pigeon
Poo

Elizabeth Baguley

Mark Chambers

LITTLE TIGER PRESS
London

In a perfect town with tidy streets,

And flawless lawns with shiny seats,

A pigeon swooped and looped the loop,

And left behind a trail of . . .

Soon brollies, shoes
and smart new hats

Were spoiled by Pidge's
splots and **splats**.

A garden gnome had dreadful luck,

Some champion sunflowers dripped with muck.

When Pidge flew by he'd always drop

A massive load of pigeon **plop**.

As Pidge high-dived with loops and twists
The townsfolk frowned and shook their fists.
They stamped and shouted, full of rage:
"THAT PIGEON SHOULD BE IN A CAGE!"

They set a trap
to catch the chick

But clever Pidge
was far too quick.

Dedicated to those
who fell in the Great
Custard Battle of 1836...

He shot off to a
dizzy height
And turned a statue
gloopy white.

The townsfolk gathered
chains and strings,

Cogs and sprockets,
stretchy things.

They made a **whopping,**
Super-duper,
Snapping, zapping...

Instructions

With **sparks** and **pops**,
the **HUGE** contraption
Catapulted into action.

Pidge dodged
and dived . . .

and ducked
and flapped,
But soon, poor thing,
was firmly . . .

But one girl cried, "HE SHOULD BE FREE!
I'll save our town – leave this to me!"

And soon our Pidge was clean and happy

In a bird-sized, poop-proof . . .

You'll be flying high with these Little Tiger books!

Boris's Big Bogey
Paul Bright
Hannah George

Dragon Stew

The Not-So Scary Snorklum
Paul Bright Jane Chapman

What a Mess!
Adria Meserve

The Slurpy Burpy Bear
Norbert Landa
Jane Chapman

with fold-out pages
MY MONSTER DUMPER TRUCK
Steve Smallman Joëlle Dreidemy

For information regarding any of the above titles or for our catalogue, please contact us:

Little Tiger Press, 1 The Coda Centre, 189 Munster Road, London SW6 6AW

Tel: 020 7385 6333 • Fax: 020 7385 7333 • E-mail: info@littletiger.co.uk • www.littletigerpress.com